Winnie Wagtail

Neil Griffiths

Illustrated by Eileen Browne

Winnie, like all lively puppies,
loved to play!

She loved to ...

... nip and nibble ...

... pounce and
bounce ...

... howl and growl ...

... hide and slide.

She loved to snuffle with her wet nose, peep with her sparkling eyes and listen with her eager ears.

But, unlike other young puppies, Winnie couldn't quite get the hang of wagging her tail.

She'd try her hardest to wag it, but usually her bottom just swayed in the air ...

... and her tiny tail didn't wag at all.

Her mother told Winnie not to worry. "You'll soon learn how to do it," she said gently. "All puppies' tails wag eventually."

But Winnie wanted it to wag now!

Winnie wandered off grumpily
through the farmyard,
muttering to herself.

In the paddock she
watched as the horse
swished its tail.

"I wish I could swish *my* tail," she said.

But when she tried, her bottom just swayed and her little tail didn't swish at all.

"Puppies don't swish, they wag!" laughed the horse.

Winnie wandered
on to the orchard
and watched as
the donkey
twirled its tail.

"I wish I could twirl my tail," she said.
But when she tried, her bottom just swayed and her little tail didn't twirl at all.

"Puppies don't twirl, they wag!" chuckled the donkey.

Winnie wandered on further to the bottom of the hill and watched the sheep **twitching** its tail.

"I wish I could twitch my tail," she said. But when she tried, her bottom just swayed and her little tail didn't twitch at all.

Winnie wandered even further to the edge of the meadow and watched the cow **flick** its tail.

"I wish I could flick *my* tail," she said. But when she tried, her bottom just swayed and her little tail didn't flick at all.

"Puppies don't flick, they wag!" sniggered the cow.

Winnie wandered further still to the bridge that crossed the stream and watched the duck **wiggle** its tail.

"I wish I could wiggle *my* tail," she said.

But when
she tried,
her bottom
just swayed
and her little tail
didn't wiggle at all.

"Puppies don't
wiggle, they wag!"
tittered the duck.

Winnie was tired. She didn't want to wander anymore. Winnie wanted her *mum*. But where was her *mum*?

Winnie looked everywhere, but she couldn't see *mum*. Winnie began to cry. She really wanted her *mum*. Where could she be? Winnie's *mum* was always there.

Just then Winnie heard a bark in the distance.

It was her *mum!* She knew that bark anywhere. The bark got louder and louder and suddenly there she was racing towards her.

Winnie was so pleased to see her. Her *mum* licked her all over.

"Look," said Winnie's mum,
"Your tail! It's wagging.
I told you it would!"

"My tail's wagging?"
asked Winnie.

"Yes, look!" said all the farm animals excitedly ...

... swishing, twirling, twitching, flicking and wiggling their own tails.

"It's **wagging!**"

"But I didn't try to wag it," said Winnie.
"I was just so glad to see you!"

"That's when it wags the most!"
said her mum.
"My little Winnie Wagtail! That's
what I'll call you," she grinned.

Winnie was so happy, her tail
wagged and wagged and
hasn't stopped wagging since!

. . . until his pesky family,
the Gumboyles, turned up.

"I suppose they will make themselves ill again and I'll have to look after them as usual," said Dr. Dog.

So he set
off into the
jungle to look
for herbal
medicines.

During his search he met the long-lost herbal scientist,
Professor Dash Hund.

The Professor was hunting for a rare and dangerous plant,
the Nosenip Terriblanus.

He showed Dr. Dog his tropical herb garden
and explained the healing power of each plant.

At the back of the garden, Professor Hund
suddenly spotted a trail of nosenip slime.

"Oh no!" said Dr. Dog.

"It's leading
straight back to
the Gumboyle
camp."

"Oooh, aren't they sweet,"
said Ma, as Dr. Dog and
Professor Hund came
racing into
the camp.

"STOP PLAYING
WITH THEM
THIS MINUTE!"
said Dr. Dog. "They are
highly dangerous!"

But it was too late. Kurt stood in some nosenip poo.

The poo-flies bit him badly!

"These are mosquito bites," said Dr. Dog.

"Garlic juice will stop the itching," said Professor Hund.

They rubbed some on.
Kurt was very relieved.

Fiona had been sunbathing on a nosenip without any sun block!

"Silly girl," said Dr. Dog, "you are badly burnt!"

"Sap from an aloe plant will work wonders,"
said Professor Hund.

"Ooh, that's better," said Fiona.

Gerty had been skipping with
the nosenips.

She felt sick.

Yuck!

"Motion sickness is caused by your food sloshing about in your tummy," said Dr. Dog.

"A little ginger tea will settle that,"
said Professor Hund.

Kev had been bronco riding on a nosenip.
He sat on one of the spines . . .

. . . and got a
spot on his bot.

"That's not a spot," said Dr. Dog.
"It's a nice, juicy boil full of pus!"

"A paste of
dried marigold
petals will soon
draw it out,"
said Professor
Hund.

Very slowly, the
boil got bigger . . .

and bigger . . .

AND
BIGGER!

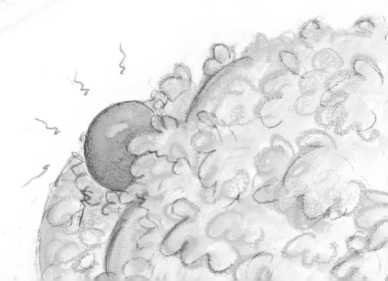

And very quickly, the nosenips got hungrier . . .

and hungrier . . .

AND HUNGRIER!

Suddenly one of them struck.

It got Baby Gumboyle!

Luckily, Kev's boil burst at that very moment.
The nosenip spat Baby out!

SPLOSH

Kev felt so
much better.

"Right, that's it," said Ma Gumboyle.
"We're NEVER going on holiday again!"

"Good job, too!"
said Dr. Dog.

To Dr. Dog

A DOSE OF DR. DOG
A RED FOX BOOK 978 0 099 48768 5

First published in Great Britain by Jonathan Cape,
an imprint of Random House Children's Books
A Random House Group Company

Jonathan Cape edition published 2007
Red Fox edition published 2008

1 3 5 7 9 10 8 6 4 2

Red Fox Books are published by Random House Children's Books,
61–63 Uxbridge Road, London W5 5SA

www.kidsatrandomhouse.co.uk
www.rbooks.co.uk

Addresses for companies within The Random House Group Limited can be found at: www.randomhouse.co.uk/offices.htm

THE RANDOM HOUSE GROUP Limited Reg. No. 954009.

A CIP catalogue record for this book is available from the British Library.

Printed in Singapore